This

TW🦉 HOOTS

book belongs to:

....

To Baba

An inspiring dad and awesome
grandpa who never, ever gives up.

First published 2016 by Two Hoots
an imprint of Pan Macmillan
20 New Wharf Road, London N1 9RR
Associated companies throughout the world www.panmacmillan.com
ISBN 978-1-4472-8662-2 (HB) ISBN 978-1-4472-8665-3 (PB)
Text and illustrations copyright © Zehra Hicks 2016. Moral rights asserted.

1 3 5 7 9 8 6 4 2
A CIP catalogue record for this book is available from the British Library.
Printed in China
The illustrations in this book were created using ink, pencil, pastel, paint and collage . . .
and a bit of Photoshop. Toilet roll rocket by Billy (age 7) and Zadie (age 5).
Extra hand lettering by Billy.

Thank you to my editor Suzanne Carnell and designer Lorna Scobie.

www.twohootsbooks.com

Flying Lemurs

Zehra Hicks

TWO HOOTS

Lemurs are really good at jumping. Everyone in my family is brilliant at it.

Mum does a great trapeze jump!

Even Granny can jump!
Her cannon jump is superb.

Dad's masterpiece is
his trampoline jump.

It's my turn next. It's going to be the most amazing jump **ever!**

Three...

Uh-oh!

I can't do it.

Don't worry.
There are lots
of other jumps
you can do.

What about the
see-saw jump?

I'll do it with you!

Oh yes, I love the see-saw jump!
There's really nothing to it.

All I have to do is stand still
and wait for Granny.

One...

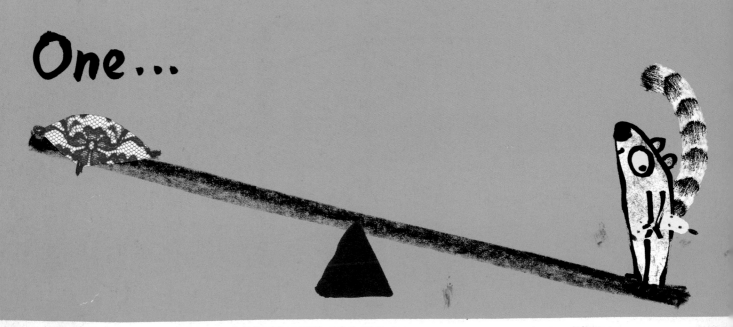

Two...

Come on Granny!

munch!
munch!

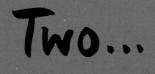

Three...

Here she
comes . . .

Uh-oh!

I can't do it.
(Sorry Granny.)

Don't worry. What about the hoops?
You're good at the hoops.

Oh yes, they're really easy.
Anyone can jump through a hoop!

Don't worry. You don't have to jump.
There are lots of other things you're good at.

You're really good at having
the fluffiest ever tail . . .

You're brilliant at playing
the tambourine . . .

And you're fantastic at throwing custard pies.

Yes, I suppose I am quite good at having the fluffiest ever tail

playing the tambourine

and throwing custard pies.

Splat!

Splat!

Splat!

In fact I'm quite good
at skateboarding too

and playing the
recorder upside down.

And I bet I can be a
really amazing rocket ...

Three... Get ready.

Two... Stretch up!

One... Bend the knees and . . .

That's the most amazing jump
ever!